You Can't CUDDLE A CROCODILE

For Freya,
with love from Granny
D.H.

For Theodore and Nancy,
my little monkeys! xx
E.E.

First published in 2019 by Hodder Children's Books

Text copyright © Diana Hendry 2019
Illustrations copyright © Ed Eaves 2019

Hodder Children's Books
An imprint of Hachette Children's Group
Part of Hodder & Stoughton
Carmelite House, 50 Victoria Embankment
London, EC4Y 0DZ

A catalogue record of this book is available from the British Library.

HB ISBN: 978 1 444 92454 1
PB ISBN: 978 1 444 92455 8

1 3 5 7 9 10 8 6 4 2
Printed in China

An Hachette UK Company
www.hachette.co.uk
www.hachettechildrens.co.uk

FSC
www.fsc.org

MIX
Paper from
responsible sources
FSC® C104740

*Hodder
Children's
Books*

YOU CAN'T CUDDLE A CROCODILE

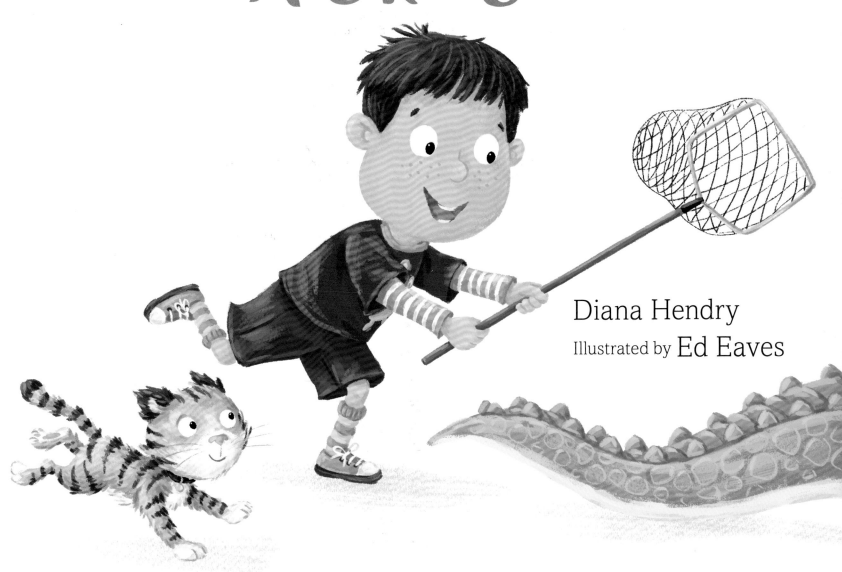

Diana Hendry

Illustrated by Ed Eaves

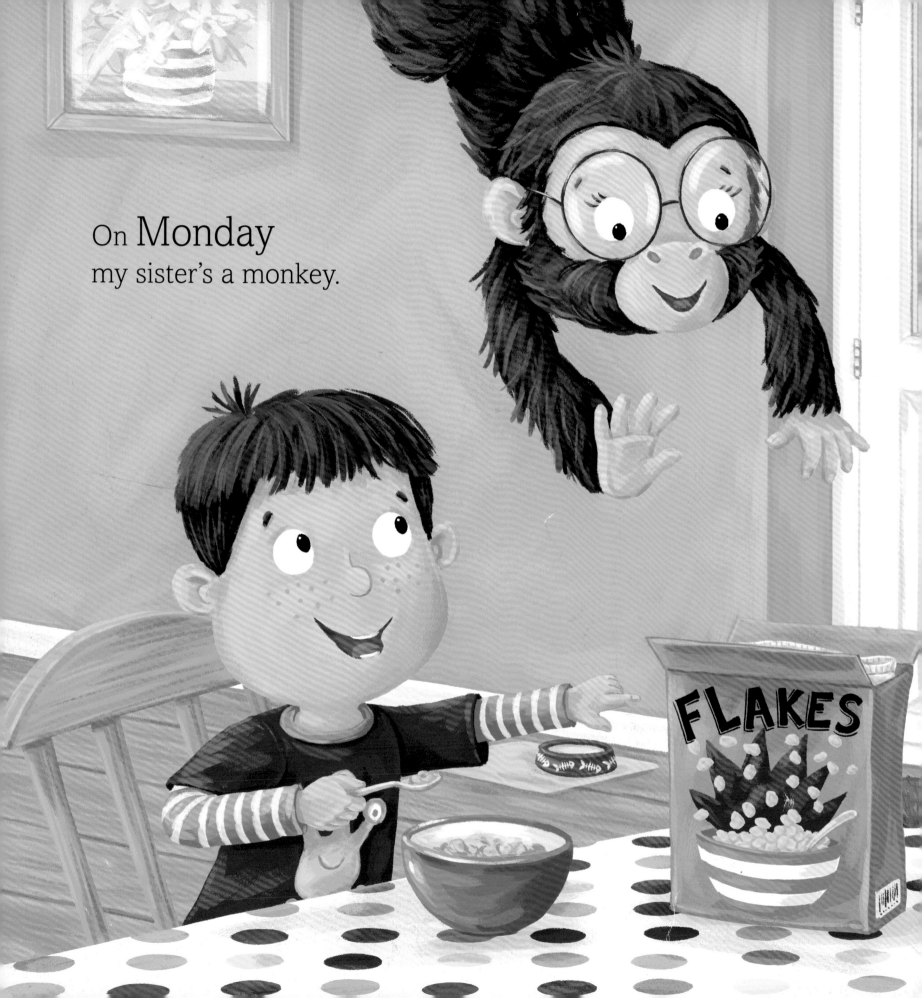

On Monday
my sister's a monkey.

"I wonder what monkeys eat for breakfast?" asks Mum.

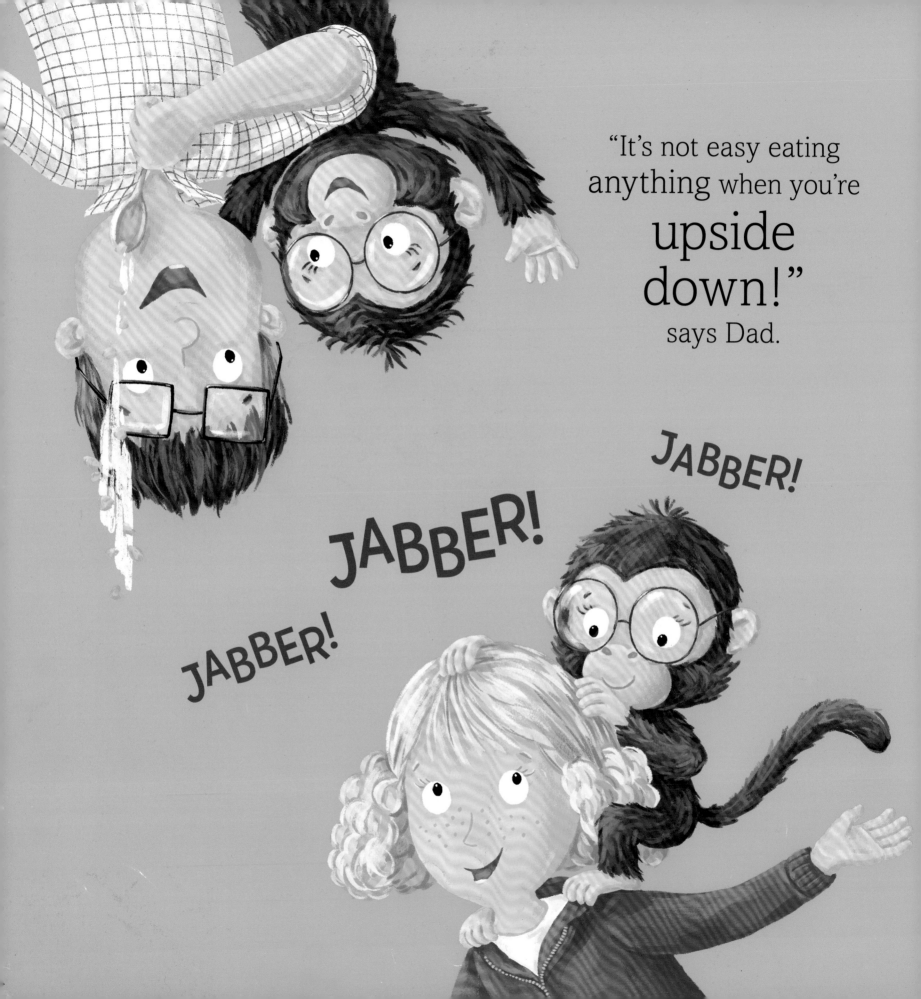

"It's not easy eating anything when you're **upside down!**" says Dad.

JABBER!

JABBER!

JABBER!

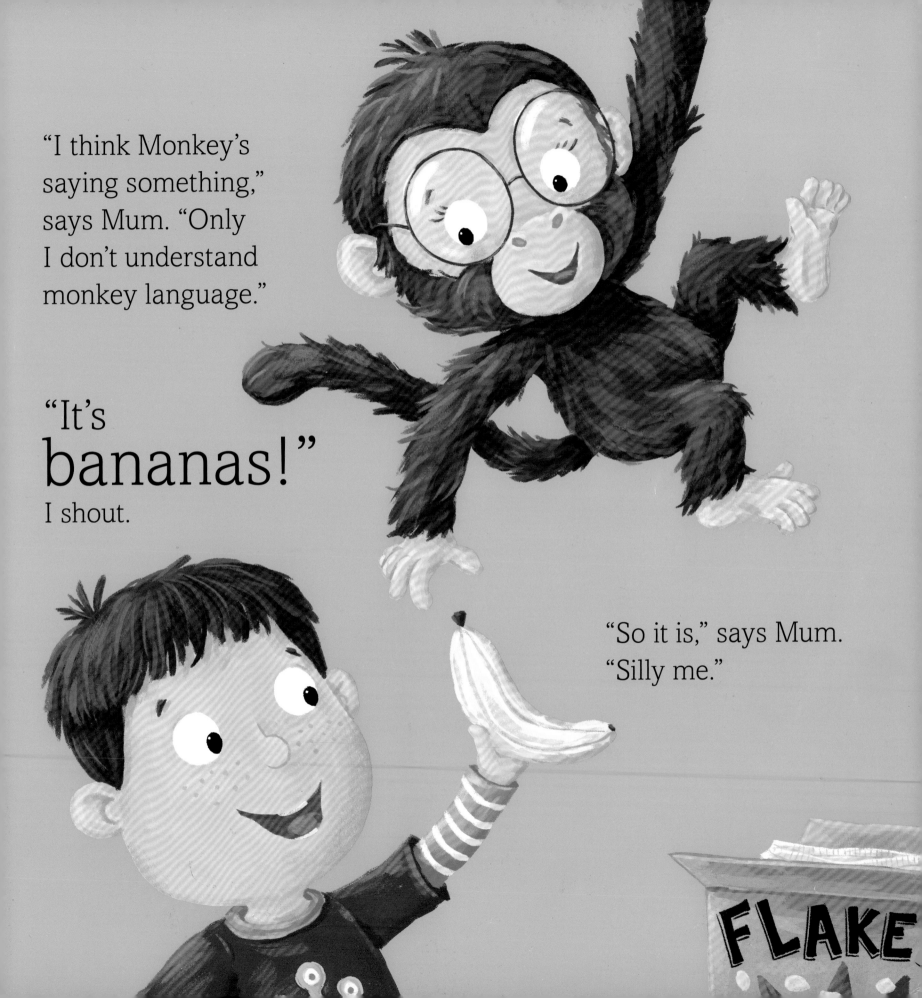

"I think Monkey's saying something," says Mum. "Only I don't understand monkey language."

"It's **bananas!**" I shout.

"So it is," says Mum. "Silly me."

FLAKE

On **Tuesday** my sister's a bear.

"Please, no more hugs!" says Mum.
"I need to do the washing up."

"Whoops!" says Dad. "I think I've just tripped over a sulky bear."

GRRRRR!

On Wednesday
Mum takes us to the beach.

My sister's a camel.

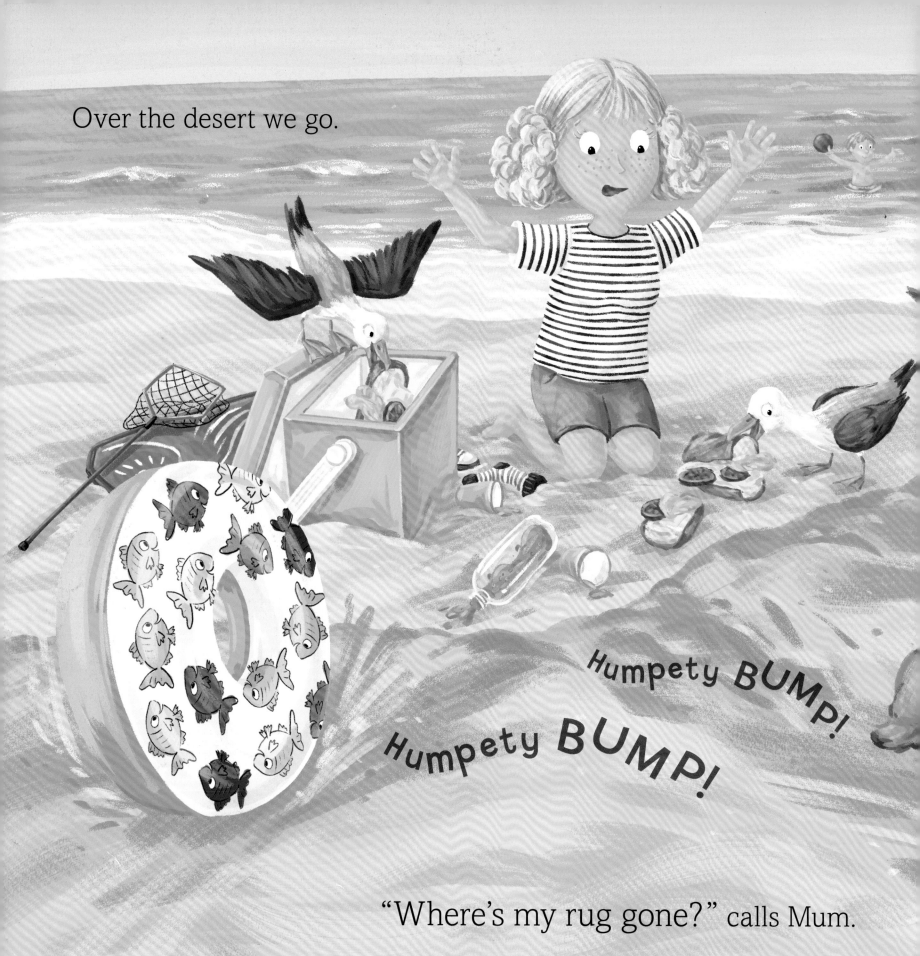

Over the desert we go.

Humpety BUMP!

Humpety BUMP!

"Where's my rug gone?" calls Mum.

On **Thursday** we go shopping in the rain.

"Is there something the matter with your sister?" asks the shopkeeper. "She's got very odd feet."

"I don't have a sister," I say . . .

"I've got a penguin!"

Shopping takes a long time
when you have flippers.

But sliding is faster.

On Friday
Dad reads us a bedtime story.
My sister's a crocodile.

"Oh dear," says Dad. "I do miss my little girl.
You can't cuddle a crocodile."

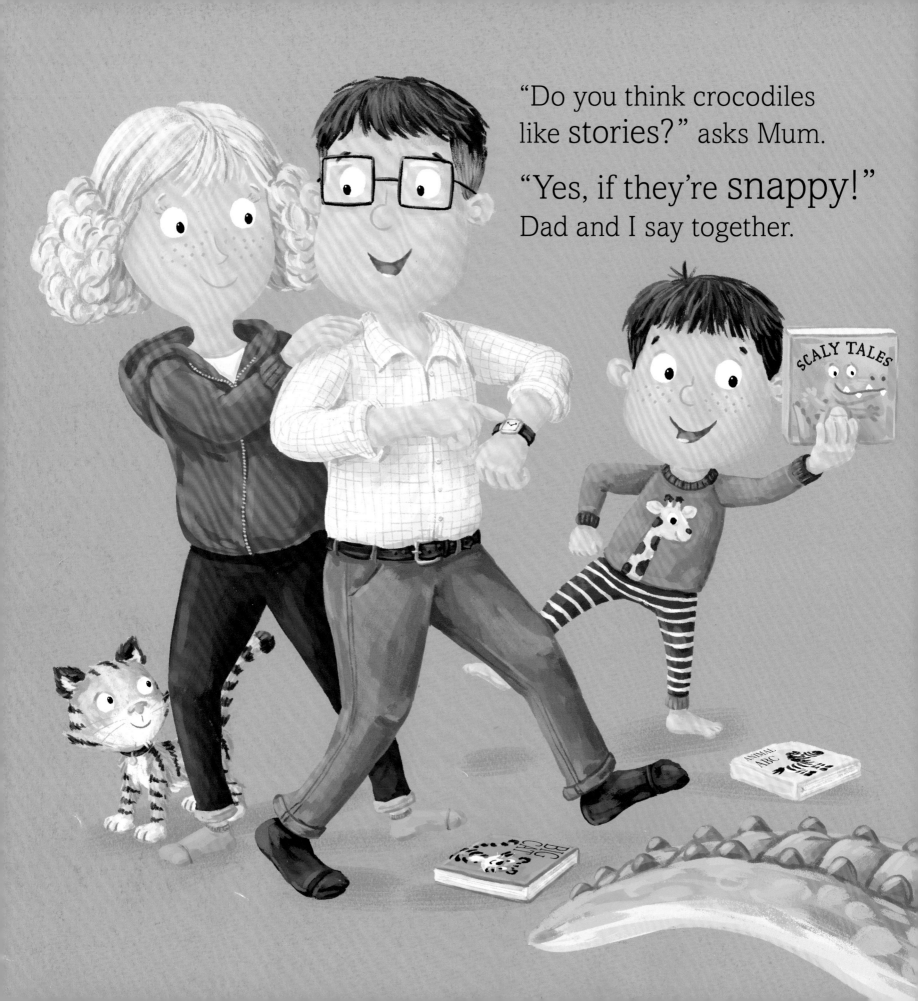

"Do you think crocodiles like stories?" asks Mum.

"Yes, if they're snappy!" Dad and I say together.

On **Saturday** my sister's a lion.
She goes prowling about the garden, roaring.

ROAR!
ROAR!

The postman looks very scared.

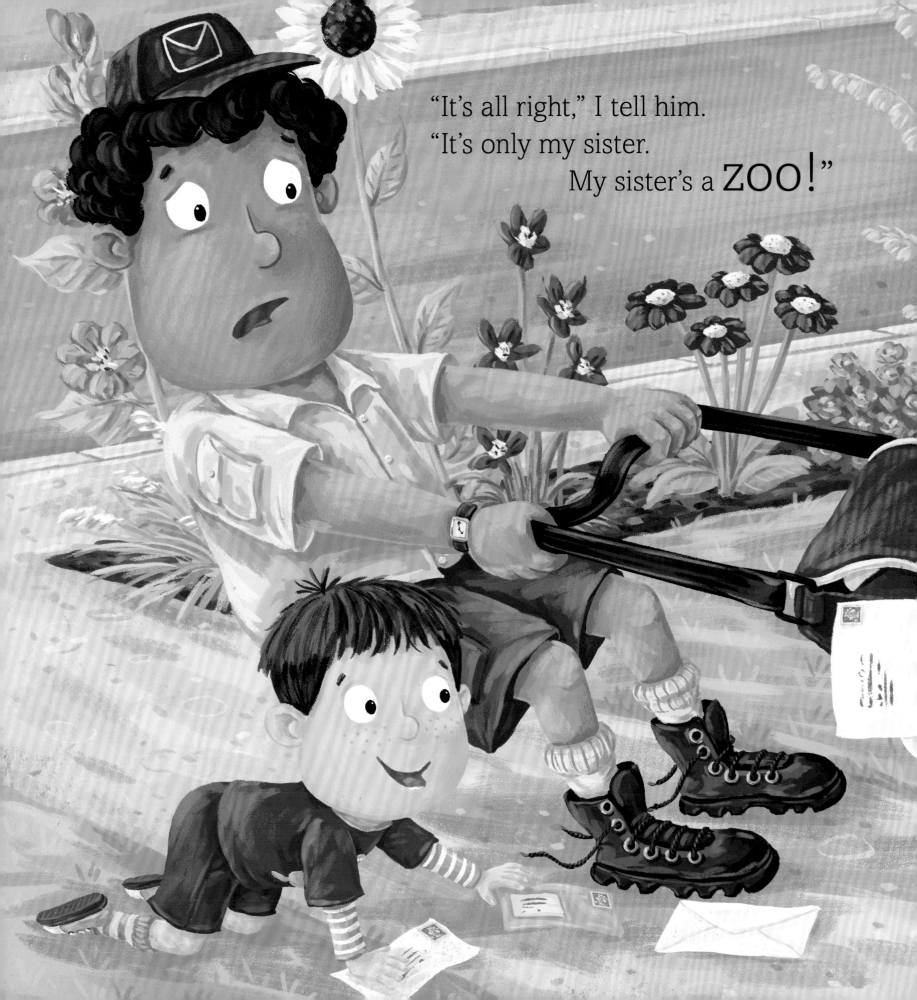

"It's all right," I tell him.
"It's only my sister.
My sister's a ZOO!"

"I liked it better when she was your sister," the postman says.

"So did I," I say.

But on Sunday . . .

. . . my sister's my sister again.

She's **Freya** all day long.

"Oh!" says Mum.
"You're **back!**
Welcome home.
Where's your brother?"

"He's up in the garden," says my sister.

I'm a giraffe!

Who's got the
last laugh?